Clifford's TRICKS

Story and pictures by Norman Bridwell

SCHOLASTIC INC.
New York Toronto London Auckland Sydney Tokyo

For Eric Shawn and Brian Matthew

ISBN 0-590-33612-6

12 11 10 9 8 7 6 5 4   7 8 9/8 0 1/9

Printed in the U.S.A.   24

Whee! A new family moved in next door.

They have a girl, and the girl has a dog.

The girl said, "Hi, I'm Martha, and this is
my dog, Bruno. He's a very big dog."

I said, "I'm Emily Elizabeth.

This is my dog, Clifford. He's big, too."

"Well," Martha said, "your dog may be a little bigger than Bruno, but I bet Bruno is smarter. I will show you some tricks."

Then Martha sent Bruno to the newspaper stand to bring her a paper.

So I sent Clifford to bring ME a paper.

Martha said, "Bruno plays dead better than any dog I know." He was pretty good —

but not as good as Clifford.

"That was pretty good," Martha said.

"But watch this."

Martha said, "Speak, Bruno."

Bruno spoke.

I hated to do it,

but I couldn't let Clifford lose.

I said, "Speak, Clifford."

BOW

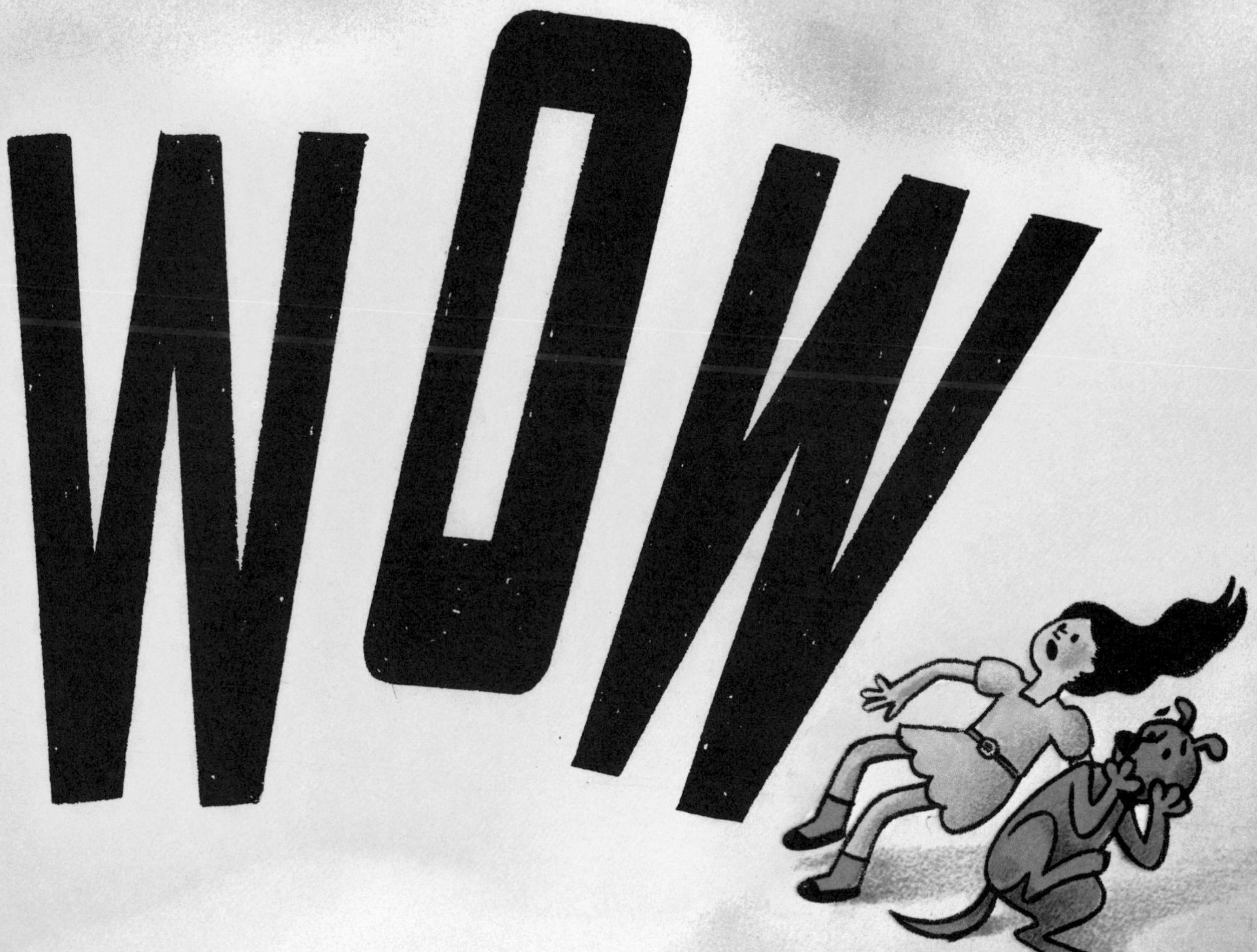
WOW

Some people
make such a fuss
over a little bark.

I told the policemen I wouldn't let Clifford

bark again. I told them it was just a trick.

They wanted to see Clifford do another trick.

So I told him to roll over.

That was a mistake.

We decided to take a walk while the policemen
talked to Daddy about the car.

Martha said, "Maybe Clifford is a little bigger and a little smarter, but I bet Bruno is braver."

We walked to the bridge.

"I'll show you how brave Bruno is," Martha said.

She told Bruno to jump on the railing and walk.

He was too smart. He wouldn't do it.

Then Martha did a foolish thing.

She got up on the railing to show Bruno

how easy it was.

But she slipped.

Bruno was brave. He jumped in to save her.

But he just wasn't big enough

or strong enough.

HELP! HELP! HELP!

It was Clifford. Hooray!

The policemen were so happy

that they forgave Clifford for mashing their car.

Martha said, "Thank you, Clifford.

You are the biggest, bravest, smartest dog I know."

Now we both know who is the best dog of all.